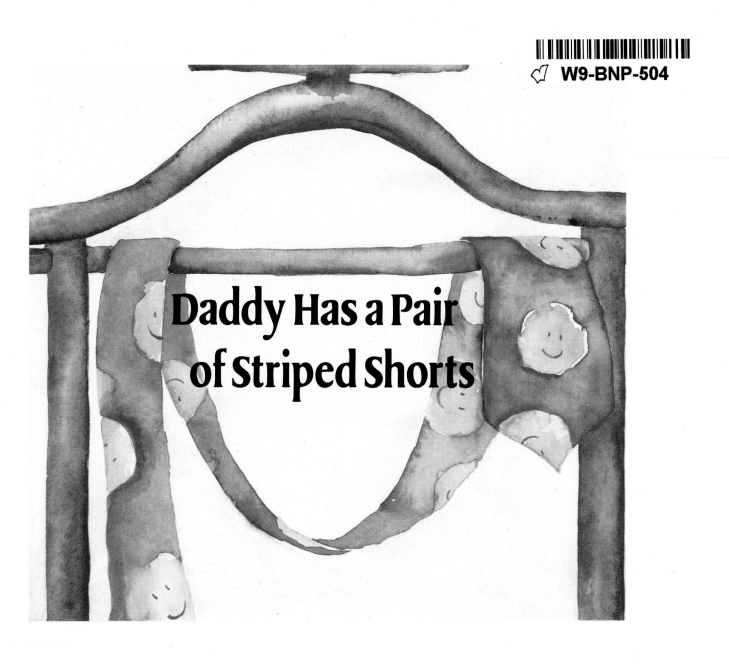

Daddy Has a Pair
of Striped Shorts

Mimi Otey

Daddy Has a Pair of Striped Shorts

HOUGHTON MIFFLIN COMPANY

BOSTON

Atlanta   Dallas   Geneva, Illinois

Palo Alto   Princeton   Toronto

Daddy has a pair of striped shorts

that he wears with his Hawaiian shirt

9

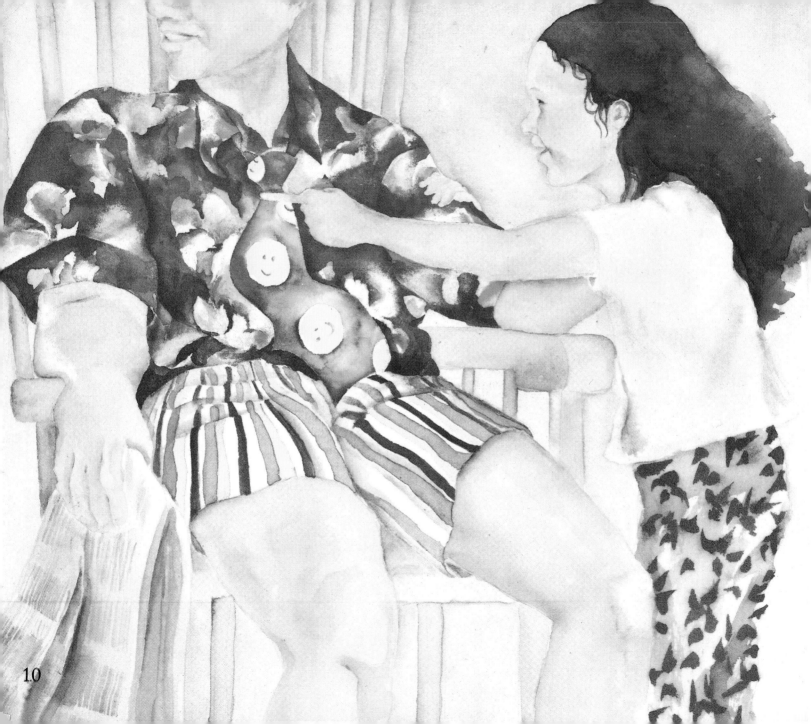

and his smiley-face tie.

Uncle Leon says Daddy has a real flair for dressing.

12

Mama says that he is color-blind.

My brother John and I. . . .we think he just has bad taste.

And sometimes it's embarrassing.

Daddy believes in supporting the PTA.

And he likes to know who our teachers are.

ADVENTURES OF DO
- PG -

NOW SHOWING

Daddy also believes in Sunday matinees,

and family night at Morrison's cafeteria.

Daddy thinks it's important to meet our new friends

and their parents.

On Saturdays, he comes early to pick us up from swim class.

POOL RULES
1. NO RUNNING
2. NO HORSEPLAYING
3. NO DUNKING
4. NO DIVING
   BELOW 5 FEET

He always has lots to say about perfecting the butterfly stroke.

On top of all this,

Daddy is a preacher.

Once in a while, he manages to blend in.

But most of the time he just stands out.

Funny, how people seem to like him no matter what he wears

or how bright it is.

And now that I've been thinking about it,

so do I.